IRISH FAIRY STORIES FOR CHILDREN

Irish Fairy Stories for Children

EDMUND LEAMY

ILLUSTRATED BY

FRANK & GAIL DOWLING

ᏜᎬᎡᏟᏆᎬᎡ ᏢᎡᎬᏕᏕ

MERCIER PRESS
PO Box 5, 5 French Church Street, Cork
16 Hume Street, Dublin 2

This selection © Mercier Press, 1979

ISBN 1 85635 008 8

A CIP record is available for this book from the British Library.

13 12 11 10 9 8 7 6 5 4

Printed in Ireland by Colour Books Ltd.

Contents

Contents

The Fairy Minstrel of Glenmalure

I

The Little Minstrel

Kathleen and Eamonn were under the beech tree that stood in the hollow down near the stream. Kathleen sat against the tree trunk, stitching the sleeve of her dolly's dress. Eamonn was lying on his back, his hands under his head, his cap down on his forehead, and his eyes closed.

'Eamonn, do you believe,' asked Kathleen, 'that there are any real live fairies now?'

'I don't know,' said Eamonn, scarcely moving his lips.

Just then a beech nut fell and hit him on the nose. He opened his eyes, started up, looked above him, and saw, sitting on the fork of the tree, a little man, about twice the size of your finger. He wore a little, three-cornered black

7

hat with a red plume in it, a little black coat and a red waistcoat, a little yellow knee-breeches and white stockings, and little black shoes with gold buckles.

'Oh! you don't, don't you?' said the little man. And, without another word, he took a little reed out of his pocket and began to blow from it bubble after bubble as beautiful as the wing of a dragonfly in the sunlight.

'Are they soap bubbles, Eamonn?' asked Kathleen.

'Soap bubbles!' returned Eamonn. 'How could they be soap bubbles, you goosie? Sure, he has no soap, and he has no water.'

Then the little man blew another bubble, still more beautiful, which was about half as big as himself. He hopped on to this, and the bubble floated away with him over the meadow and across the stream and up into the wood.

'Well, in all my born days, I never saw the like of that before,' said a magpie that had flown down close to where the children were. But they had not seen him, so engaged were they in watching the little fairy man sailing way.

'Oh, Eamonn,' said Kathleen, 'look! There is a single magpie.'

'There are some little girls that I know,' said

another voice, 'who are in a very great hurry to speak sometimes.'

And Mrs Magpie hopped down beside Mr Mag.

'There are two magpies now,' said Eamonn, 'and two are for luck.'

'True for you,' said Mr Mag, 'and both of you are in luck today.'

'Who was that little man?' said Eamonn to the Mag.

'He is Fardarrig, the fairy minstrel of Glenmalure,' said the Mag.

'And what tune was he playing?' asked Kathleen.

'He was playing *The Wind in the Reeds*,' answered Mrs Mag. 'It is a very sweet tune, but it is very sad, and it always makes me cry,' said she, while a tear dropped from her eye. 'Dear me,' she went on, 'I am sorry I left my little lace handkerchief at home,' and she put her head under her wing to dry her tears.

Mr Mag chuckled, and got a fit of coughing that almost choked him. When he recovered, he said:

'It is a sad tune, indeed. But, oh! if you could hear him playing *The Bees among the Blossoms* you would never tire of listening to it.'

'Where could we hear him playing that?' asked Eamonn.

'If you go round there to the sunny side of the wood,' said the Mag, 'and go in through the first mossy pathway you meet, maybe you won't be long till you find him.'

'Oh, come on, Eamonn!' said Kathleen.

And the children ran off, hand-in-hand, as fast as they could.

When they were gone, Mrs Mag began to peck and peep around the foot of the beech tree.

'Dear me!' said she, 'how forgetful some children are, to be sure.'

'Why, what have you got there?' said Mr Mag.

'Kathleen's silver thimble, which she left after her.'

'Well, there is no use in leaving it there after you,' said he.

'No,' said Mrs Mag, 'and you would never know when it would come in useful.'

Snatching up the thimble, she and Mr Mag, like the pair of thieves that they were, flew off to their nest.

In the meantime, the children had got round to the sunny side of the wood, and they soon came to a pathway that was all aglow in the sunshine. They ran up this till a little rabbit ran across their way.

'Oh, let us catch the rabbit, Kathleen!' cried Eamonn.

And the two rushed after the rabbit, when, all of a sudden, they heard a voice saying:

'Oh, botheration to you, for a little rabbit, you nearly knocked me down.' And who was it that spoke but one of the nicest little old Grannies you could see in a day's walk. She had a little three-legged stool in her right hand.

'Dearie me,' said she, addressing the children. "'Tis I am glad to see you, darlings, and now will you come and help me find my little Kerry cow with the black silk coat and the silver horns?'

'Oh! we will indeed,' said the children, and the three tripped away together.

'I hear someone whispering over there,' said Kathleen.

'That is the stream whispering to the brambles,' said Eamonn.

'I hear a little weeny bell,' said Kathleen.

'That's the Kerry,' said the little woman. And they had not gone far when they saw the little cow.

'Oh, Eamonn! Eamonn! did you ever see

such a little moo cow? She would almost fit in my Noah's Ark,' said Kathleen; and no wonder she said it, for the cow was only a little bigger than their black pussy-cat at home, and each of her silver horns was nearly as long as herself.

When the Kerry saw them, she trotted up.

'Well! Well! What a lot of trouble you have given me,' said the little woman. 'Go straight home before me now.' And the little cow went on crying 'moo, moo-oo', while her little bell kept tinkling.

'Is she saying "I'm sorry"?' asked Kathleen.

'Oh, she is very ready to say that,' said the little woman.

'And does she really be sorry?' returned Kathleen.

'Not always, I'm afraid,' said Granny.

'That's the way with a little girl I know,' said Eamonn.

'I hope he does not mean you, Kathleen,' said the little woman.

'No; it's another little girl that we play with sometimes,' said Kathleen.

By this time, they had come up near Granny's cottage, and the little cow stopped in front of the lovely little summerhouse, covered all over with creepers and beautiful blue and white and golden-coloured flowers. Then the little woman put down the stool and the little milking-pail.

'Now, Miss Kathleen,' said she, 'would you like to milk my little Kerry cow?'

'Will you show me how?' asked Kathleen.

The little woman did, and then Kathleen began to milk; and the little cow was so pleased that she never switched her tail – although the midges were tormenting her – lest she might frighten Kathleen.

Suddenly they heard the sound of music. Eamonn looked to see where it came from, and what should he see but the little fairy minstrel of Glenmalure sitting on a ferny bank playing on his little reed.

'Oh, what is he playing now?' asked Eamonn.

'He is playing *Cailín deas cruidhte na mbó* "The pretty girl milking the cows".'

'I never heard that before,' said Eamonn.

'Of course you never did,' said Granny, 'nor did anyone else. He is making it up now in honour of Miss Kathleen; but it will be sung everywhere yet all over Erin by the milkmaids in the sunset on the summer eves.'

Well, when the cow was milked –

'Come with me now into the summerhouse,' said the little woman. 'I have the nicest griddle-bread you ever tasted, and the biggest and the sweetest blackberries, and you never drank any cream that is half so rich as this milk.'

'Could the little minstrel man come with us?' asked Eamonn.

'My darling boy,' cried the little woman, 'that's the very thing I would like, for I never let a minstrel pass my door, and have never sent one empty-handed away.'

'Can we both go and bring him in?' asked Kathleen.

'Of course, dearest,' said the little woman, kissing Kathleen, 'and I'll go and get ready the griddle-bread.'

The two children ran towards the little minstrel, who popped down from the bank and doffed his little plumed cap.

'Will you come and lunch with ourselves and Granny?' said Kathleen.

'I shall be delighted, my lady,' said the little man, bowing almost to the ground. He walked between the two children, who kept well out from him lest they might tread on him; for he was hardly as high as the top of Eamonn's boot.

As they entered the summerhouse, the little

woman cried: 'Welcome, and welcome again, Fardarrig!'

Then the whole four of them sat down at the table; but two chairs had to be set for the little man, one on top of the other, so as to bring him above the level of the table.

The children said they had never tasted such griddle-bread in their lives, and as to the blackberries, they were as big as plums and melted in the mouth. The cream, too, was simply delicious, and when they had partaken of these, the little woman said:

'Dearie me! there is something I forgot. Could you guess, Kathleen, what it is?'

'I don't know,' said Kathleen, 'unless it is honey.'

'The very thing,' said Granny, 'and I am so sorry.'

'I know what I would like,' said Eamonn, looking shyly at the little minstrel.

'And what is it?' asked Granny.

'I would like to hear another tune from the little minstrel.'

'Oh, you would, would you?' said Fardarrig, blushing, and quite pleased. 'What would you like?'

'Will you play *The Bees among the*

Blossoms?' asked Eamonn.

'With the greatest pleasure,' said the little minstrel, and he took out the little reed from his pocket.

At first, the children could scarcely hear any sound, but the most wonderful perfume filled the summerhouse as of numberless sweet-scented flowers. But soon they began to hear a faint drowsy hum, something like that which they were wont to hear up in the top boughs of the sweet-blossomed lime tree that grew near their house. As they listened, the sound seemed to come nearer and nearer, and to shape itself into the most exquisite melody. As it sank into their ears and into their hearts, the children stood as if they were fascinated, their eyes wide open watching the little man. They hardly dared to breathe lest they might miss a note of the bewitching music. And they would have so stood for ever, if the little man had not finished playing and put the reed in his pocket.

Then he popped off the chair, and he said:

'I must be going. I see a crow out there from Glenmalure. I know he is from Glenmalure by the twist of his tail, and if I catch him in time he will give me a lift home. So goodbye to you all now, and may good luck attend you and bles-

17

sings shower down on you, but don't come further with me than the door, lest the crow would hear you, and take himself off.'

When they came to the door, the little minstrel doffed his plumed cap and kissed goodbye to Kathleen. Then he trod lightly on the tops of the blades of grass until he came to where the crow was pecking away. Before the crow knew where he was, my bold little minstrel hopped up, stretched himself flat on his back, and put his head on the crow's poll, which made him a very comfortable pillow.

'Caw! caw! caw!' said the crow. And up he flew to where a long line of other crows were sailing away between the south and the west, and he followed after them. As he went up, the little man once more took the reed from his pocket and began to play, and the fairy music floated down to the children.

'He is playing again,' said Kathleen.

'He is,' said Eamonn, 'and I know what he is playing.'

'What is it?' asked the little woman.

'*Over the Hills and Far Away*,' said Eamonn. And it was.

II

The Little Outlaws

Then Granny and the children went back again into the summerhouse.

'Oh, my!' said Kathleen, as she saw the table.

'Honey, Eamonn! Honey! Where do you think it came from?'

'Where do *you* think it came from?' asked the little woman.

'I don't know,' replied Kathleen.

'Neither do I,' said Eamonn, 'unless it was the bees amongst the blossoms that we heard in the little man's music that brought it to us.'

'You have guessed right, Eamonn, asthore,' said she.

'But why did we not see the bees?' asked Kathleen.

'Because you could not take your eyes off the fairy minstrel's face,' said the little woman.

'That's really true,' said Kathleen. 'I thought my eyes were fastened to his.'

'I thought so, too,' said Eamonn.

Well, then, they had the honey, and such

honey! No mortal children had ever tasted its like before.

When they had eaten it, the children whispered to each other, and Granny noticed them:

'What is it?' she asked, 'speak out and don't be afraid.'

The children looked at each other shyly, and then Eamonn said with a smile:

'We would like to take some of it home to little mother.'

'We would,' said Kathleen. 'We always like to bring her home flowers and sweets, and everything that's nice.'

'You shall bring her home the honey too,' said Granny.

And from a little cupboard in the corner she took two dainty little baskets, woven of green fragrant rushes. She packed the honeycombs in every so neatly.

'Now,' said she, 'I am sure you would like to get home to your little mother.'

'We would,' said Kathleen, 'and we thank you for a very happy day.'

'I can only go a little bit of the way with you,' said Granny, 'for I want to take some milk to a poor lone widow who lives on the side of the mountain; but I will put you on the right track, and when you are once on it, don't stop to look at anything, or maybe you'd get into trouble.'

The three started off from the summerhouse, but soon they heard 'Moo! moo!' behind them, and who came trotting up but the little Kerry cow.

'She wants to come with us,' said Kathleen. 'May she?'

'She wants to do more, I think,' said Granny. 'I know her.'

'What is it?' asked Kathleen.

Before Granny could answer, the little Kerry had put one of her silver horns under the handle of Kathleen's basket, and the other under Eamonn's.

'That's what she wants – to carry the baskets for you,' said the little woman. The Kerry, as proud as possible, marched along between the two children, her little bell tinkling musically all the time. When it came to the turn where they had to part, Granny put them on the right track. She kissed them and blessed them before she said goodbye. They kissed her, and they patted and thanked the little Kerry for carrying the baskets. Then catching each other's hands, the two of them sped away.

They had not gone very far when Kathleen

saw hanging from the branch of a tree something like a long pocket or stocking.

'Oh, Eamonn, Eamonn,' she cried, pulling him by the hand, and checking him. 'What is that growing on the tree?'

'Come on, come one, did not the little woman tell you not to stop?'

'Yes; but what is it?' said Kathleen.

'I think it is a wasp's nest,' said Eamonn.

It was, but what was worse still, the wasps had caught the delicious scent of the honey, and they swarmed out of the nest in thousands round the children, and their angry buzzing said: 'We'll sting you to death! we'll sting you to death!'

Eamonn put his arm round Kathleen's neck, and pulled her to him to try and shield her from the wasps who kept on buzzing: 'We'll sting you to death! we'll sting you to death!'

The children thought they almost felt the stings, when they heard a voice crying:

'Will you sting them to death? Charge, my gallant knights, and don't leave a wasp alive!'

Like the rush of leaves speeding before the blast, hundreds of little horsemen in silver armour, with little green silk cloaks fluttering on their shoulders, some armed with little

swords and some with lances half as long as knitting-needles, charged on the wasps, and cut and slashed and thrust at them. In a few seconds, hundreds and thousands of wasps were lying dead and dying on the ground. The little woman, hearing the noise of battle and suspecting danger to the children, rushed back and pulled them out of the thick of the fight, and told them to remember the sting of a dying wasp was worse than the sting of a live one.

When the wasps were all killed or put to flight, the little horsemen formed their ranks; and with their captain, little Prince Golden Hair, at their head, they marched towards the little woman and the children.

'Welcome, Prince Golden Hair! Welcome, my bonny outlaws of the woods of Glenmalure!' said the little woman. 'Now, after your hard fight and great victory, I am sure you all want a drink of milk, so come along and take it.'

So eager were they to get it, that they galloped right up against the little pail, and three of them fell over their horses' heads into the milk, and they would have been drowned if Granny had not been there to pull them out by the heels. Their captain, the Prince, was very much annoyed at this. He told them they should march round the pail in regular order, and as each passed by he was to dip his drinking horn into the milk.

Then each of the outlaws, taking a little silver horn from his belt, dipped it into the milk and drank it off. When all had finished, there was not a drop of milk less in the pail!

Then the little Prince spoke to Eamonn and Kathleen, and said he was glad he was in time to save their lives, and he was very sorry he could not send an escort home with them. But he could not do so, as he and his outlaws were bound to be back in Glenmalure before sunset.

'It is nearly that now,' said the little Prince, and he begged permission to kiss Kathleen's hand. Then shaking hands with Eamonn and with Granny, he ordered his trumpeters to play up a march. And to the music of their little trumpets, the fairy outlaws of Glenmalure marched up through the heather and over the hill, their little helmets glowing like rosy jewels in the light of the setting sun.

III

The Three Riddles

'Now, children,' said Granny, 'I wish I could go with you. But run as fast as ever you can, and don't look to the right or to the left until you get out of this enchanted wood. Blessings on you again, Eamonn, asthore, and on you, Kathleen, aroon,' and having hugged and kissed the two of them, she pushed them away from her, saying – 'Run for your bare lives.'

The children ran as hard as ever they could. One little turn more and they would be out of the wood. But just when they were close to this, and could see through the opening the fields and hills that they knew were near their own home, they heard a voice as of thunder and the crash of falling timber. With their hearts in their mouths they ran faster and faster, thinking it was a thunderstorm. A big tree crashed down on the pathway before them, followed by another sound as of thunder, and then a giant, almost as high as a tree, stepped out crashing and slashing the trees as he passed. It was his voice they mistook for the thunder. He had a huge club, all studded with iron bolts, and it was with this he was knocking down the trees, as a boy might knock down with his cane the weeds and thistles that came in his way. He had a huge paunch, and around it was a broad belt, and fastened to this was a wallet in which you could stow away a cow. A dead sheep was slung over his shoulders, her legs tied under his chin. He had only one eye, a horrible eye in the centre of his forehead; his nose was large, flat and broad, his nostrils as big as chimney tops, and his mouth as broad as a trap-door. Every one of his teeth was as long and as sharp as a scythe.

The children were nearly frightened to death when they saw the monster.

'Ho! ho! who have we here?' he shouted; and his voice rolled through the wood, and the trees trembled.

'Two children,' said Eamonn, 'who are going home to their little mother.'

'Home!' said the monster – 'home was never like this place!' and with one hand he grasped the two children, lifted them up, and dropped them down into his deep wallet.

When they were down in the bottom, the top

seemed as high as a house, and the sky ever so far away.

The children were too frightened to cry, but after a little while Kathleen said –

'Oh, Eamonn, what will he do? Will he eat us?'

'I don't know,' said Eamonn, 'but if little mother were here she would save us.'

'Do you think she would hear us calling her, Eamonn? You know she always heard us calling her, even when she used to be asleep.'

'But she would not know where to find us, and how would she get into this wallet? Maybe the giant would eat her, too, and we would not like that?'

'No,' said Kathleen, 'but listen Eamonn, what is that? Listen!'

They listened, and they thought they heard someone say, 'Hush! hush.' They looked about them. They could see no one in the darkness. Then they looked up to the top of the wallet, and what should they see creeping down, head foremost, like a fly on a wall, but little Fardarrig, the fairy minstrel.

'Not a word out of you; but whisper, and listen to me,' said he. 'The giant will stop soon, and sit down to have his supper. He will take the two of you out of this, and he will give you a chance for your lives. For he does that to all his prisoners. He will ask you, Eamonn, three riddles, and if you can answer all three right, he will let you go. If you can't, it will be all up with you,' said the little man, sadly.

'What are they?' said Eamonn.

'I am sorry to say,' answered the little man, 'I only know two he is sure to ask you. You must try to answer the third for yourself.'

'What are the two?' said Eamonn.

'The first is, "What is whiter than the snow of one night?" and the second is, "What is blacker than the blackest night?"'

'What are the answers to them?' asked Eamonn.

'I beg your pardon, Miss Kathleen,' said the little man, 'for whispering in the presence of a lady, but I am under a bond never to tell these answers to more than one person at the same time, and that person is under a bond never to tell them to anyone until he is asked the riddles by the giant. For if he should tell them, the giant would ask him other riddles which he could not answer, and he would be put to death.'

He whispered the two answers into

Eamonn's ear. Then he said aloud: 'I'm sorry, my poor Eamonn, I can't tell you the third answer, but if all goes to all, and you can't think of it, try and remember what children see in their dreams in the darkness. And now,' said he, 'I must go, for if the giant discovered me here, he would make me a prisoner for life. But keep up your hearts, and may blessings attend the two of you.'

The little man climbed up the wallet, and got away without the giant seeing him.

It happened as he had said. The giant stopped, and sitting down on a bank to prepare for supper, he plucked the dead sheep off his shoulder and cast it on the ground. Then he put his hand down in the wallet, brought up the children, and set them on the grass before him. Kathleen was very frightened, but Eamonn was trying to remember the answers to the riddles.

'Come now,' said the giant, 'before I cut you up for my supper, I will give you three chances for your lives. Do you know what a riddle is?' he said to Eamonn.

'I do,' said Eamonn.

'Well, I will ask you three riddles, and if you answer the three right, this club which I have stuck here in the ground will fall by itself without anyone touching it, and the moment it falls you must fly for your lives, or I might be tempted to forego my word. Are you ready?'

'Yes,' said Eamonn.

'First riddle, then,' said the giant. 'What is whiter than the snow of one night?'

'A soul without sin,' said Eamonn, repeating what the little minstrel had told him.

The giant's face became black.

'Second riddle,' he cried, in the angriest tone. 'What is blacker than the blackest night?'

'A heart without gratitude,' said Eamonn. The giant's face became blacker and blacker still.

'The third riddle,' said he, bellowing like a bull, 'and remember,' he roared, as if he wanted to frighten the wits out of poor Eamonn, 'on your answer depend your lives. What is brighter than the stars of night?'

Poor Eamonn was dumbfounded; he tried to think and to think.

'I'll give you two minutes to answer,' said the giant, and he pulled out from his pocket a watch that was as large as a frying-pan, and the face of it was as black as coal, and the hands of it were made from dead men's bones, and so also were the figures.

Kathleen nestled up to Eamonn, and the tears were stealing down her cheeks, and Eamonn was trying to think and think.

'One minute gone,' said the giant, and his voice sounded like a death-bell.

Eamonn began to think, and he thought of diamonds that he had seen sparkling; and he remembered that he thought at the time they were brighter than stars, and he was going to say diamonds, but the diamonds don't shine in the darkness, and the stars do, and make it bright. So he did not say diamonds. Then he tried to think again.

'A minute and a half gone,' said the giant, and his face grew brighter and brighter, while poor Eamonn became more downcast, and his head drooped, and his heart sank, and Kathleen leaned against him like one bruised reed against another.

'A minute and three-quarters gone,' growled the giant, and his face became brighter and brighter.

Suddenly Eamonn pushed Kathleen back from him, while still holding her hand. He drew himself up till he was as straight as an uplifted lance, and he looked the giant defiantly in the face.

'I know it,' he said, and his little voice rang clear as a silver bell. For he had thought of what the little minstrel had told him – to try and remember what children see in their dreams in the darkness.

'What is it?' groaned the giant, and his face became black again, fearing that his prey was about to be lost to him. 'What are brighter than the stars of night?'

'A mother's eyes!' said Eamonn.

The club fell of itself, and groaned as if it were alive. The roar of the disappointed giant made the wood tremble. But Eamonn, dragging Kathleen along with him, rushed like the wind. They had scarcely got outside the enchanted wood, when they heard:

'Kathleen! Kathleen! Eamonn! Eamonn! where are you?'

'Eamonn! Eamonn! that is mother!' cried Kathleen.

'Hurrah, hurrah!' shouted Eamonn, and at the sound of the dear, sweet voice, their fears and terrors left them as the nightmare leaves the sleeper, awakening to the songs of the birds and the light of the rosy morning.

'Where, where have you been, my darlings?'

'Oh, mother, mother,' said Kathleen, as the

two children were crushed together within their little mother's arms, 'Eamonn told the giant that a mother's eyes are brighter than the stars of night, and now we know – don't we, Eamonn, that her voice is sweeter than the music of the Fairy Minstrel of Glenmalure?'

The Little Red Juggler

A long, long time ago a little thatched cottage stood on the side of a steep hill and looked down through a pleasant valley. Never anywhere did the bloom of the furze take on such a deep, rich golden hue; never anywhere were the purple of the heather and the green of the bracken so restful a sight for tired eyes, and never was a valley in all the world half so fair. Down the hill a little stream danced trippingly in and out through the pebbles, and sometimes over them, flashing as brightly all the time as a merry little maiden's eyes.

Sometimes you would think it was talking to the pebbles, and sometimes you would think it was whispering to itself, but you would never tire of listening to the music of its voice. When it came down and passed through the pleasant valley, it moved so gently that you would hardly notice its motion, and its voice sank so low you would have to strain your ears to catch its tone. But you knew it was moving because of the faint rustle amongst the rushes that here and there skirted its banks.

The little hut on the side of the hill looked like a bunch of roses flung on the mingled gold of the gorse and the purple of the heather, for roses grew all over it, and when the wind of the morning stirred them they tapped at the little window that lit the room where two wee girls were sleeping in the daintiest little white cot that ever was seen. The names of the two little girls were Gladys and Monona, and they lived there all the year round with their mother, whom they loved with all their heart.

But that didn't hinder them getting fond of the furze and the heather, and of the bees and the birds and the green waving woods that clothed both sides of the valley; above all, they were fondest of the bright little stream that danced away down the hill. They had no little playmate save it. It called to them first thing in the morning; they heard it babbling away when they got into their little nest at night, and it sang them to sleep with a drowsy tune. But they were very much troubled that they could not make out what it was saying to them, for they did not doubt it was trying to talk to them, as they used to talk to it, sometimes 'hushing' it, and telling it not to be so noisy, sometimes flinging a sprig of heather or a leaf upon it, and asking how far it would carry it.

One day, when it was babbling very loudly, Gladys said:

'I wish you'd tell us what you want to say?'

'Run down there below where it dips between the boulders, and you'll learn what it is saying.'

The children looked round to see who had spoken, but they saw nothing save a yellow-hammer flying off. But they went down all the same, and sure enough when they came to where the stream bustled through the boulders they heard it saying: 'Follow me! Follow me!'

'Oh, let us follow it, Gladys,' said Monona, and away they trotted after the stream. They followed it along its banks till they were stopped by a high grey rock up which the ivy had begun to trail, but they found their way around and up through the crevices, and after a little struggle they climbed to the top of the rock, and sat down there. A thick branch of a noble elm rested on the edge of the rock, as you might rest your arm on an armchair. Another branch, nearly as thick and round, stretched out free towards the wood.

The children had hardly seated themselves

when they heard a voice saying: 'One, two, three! Here goes to Fairyland!' and they looked, and on the other branch what should they see skipping along but a little brown squirrel. When he came to the tree, he took a hazel nut that was not quite ripe out of his pocket, and he knocked three times at the tree.

'Who is there?'

The children heard a little weeny, weeny voice from inside the elm tree.

'It's Brown Coat,' said the squirrel, 'and I'm off to Fairyland!'

Then a little door, like the door of a doll's house, opened in the tree, and the little brown squirrel popped in, and the door closed after him.

Well, the two children had their mouths open all the time wondering what was to happen next, when they heard again: 'One, two, three! Here's off to Fairyland!' and what should they see but a little grey squirrel; and what did he do but go up to the tree and take a nut out of his pocket, and knock – 'Rap! rap! rap!' until the little door was opened for him, and in he popped.

'I wonder where that little fellow went to?' said Gladys.

'Of course he's gone to Fairyland,' said Monona. 'Didn't he tell us he was going there.'

'One, two, three! Here's off to Fairyland!' and the children looked round again, and there was a little white squirrel with pink eyes tapping away at the tree. In answer to the little man inside, he said he was 'White Coat', and wanted to go to Fairyland, and, when the little door was opened, in he popped.

But the door was not closed after him as it had been after the others, and the children heard the little old man inside the tree say:

'Well, well, a great many people are coming here today, and I think I might as well keep the door open and look out.'

He stepped out from the tree on to the branch.

Such a funny little old man he was! He was hardly twice as big as your thumb. He was dressed all in green velvet, save his little white stockings and his black shoes, with little silver buckles. His cap was shaped like the fingers of the fox-glove, and at the peak of it there was a peal of little fairy bells, that sounded like faintly-heard far-off music.

When he stepped on the branch, he jerked his little head this way and then that, like a perky robineen. Then he put up his hand to his eyes to shade them from the sun, which pierced through the branches of the elm, and flashed straight towards the little door in front of which he was standing. In a second he saw the children, and as soon as he did he whipped off his little cap, and the music of the bells dropped round them like a shower.

'Why, you must be two little duchesses,' he said, as he bowed almost to the ground.

'We are not duchesses, Mr Man,' said Gladys. She was going to say 'little man', but she thought he mightn't like it.

'Well, then, you must be countesses, at least.'

'We are not countesses,' said Gladys.

'Well, who in the world are you?' said the little fellow, 'for the sun is in my eyes, your ladyships.'

'We're mammy's little children,' said Monona, who plucked up courage enough to speak when she saw what a civil little man he was, but all the same she nestled under Gladys' arm.

'Well, bless my soul!' said the little fellow, 'how silly I'm getting! Of course, you are mammy's little children. Who else could you be? Didn't I often see you playing up on the hills amid the heather!' said he.

'Did you?' said Gladys. 'We never saw you.'

'Oh, that was because I wore the four-leaved shamrock,' said he, 'and that made me invisible.'

'Why did you do that?' asked Gladys.

'Because I was afraid of the bees,' said the little man, and he winked at Monona, 'and now I fear I am staying too long out here, and I must go back, but wouldn't you like to come to Fairyland for a little while?'

'Oh, we would,' cried the children together, 'but we wouldn't like to go without telling mother.'

'Can you write?' asked the little man.

'We can,' they replied.

'It's well for you,' said the little man, shaking his head very solemnly. 'I can't, for I neglected my schooling when I was young,' he said. 'I used to play truant, and instead of minding my lessons I used to go roaming through the woods and the gardens and over the moors, stealing the fruit from the beak of the blackbird, and the honey bags from the bees.'

'Is that the reason you are afraid of the bees?' said Monona.

''Tis,' said the little man, and he winked again

at Monona, and I am afraid Monona winked at him, 'but now here's notepaper for you.' He took out of his waistcoat pocket the daintiest little pocket-book ever you saw, and from this he brought out a little sheet of notepaper, no bigger than a postage stamp. He handed it to Gladys:

'Write, my lady, and tell your mother to wait for you here till you come back,' said he.

'Oh, you funny little man,' said Gladys, laughing, 'I always begin my letters, "My darling mammy", and the first letter, "M", would fill up the whole page.'

'Oh, but you never wrote with a pen like this,' said the little man, and he handed her a weeny pen with a crystal handle and a point of gold. 'Try now, my lady,' he said, and Gladys took the little pen in her hand and she tried to write a big 'M', but the little pen wouldn't do it; instead it wrote in golden ink the tiniest little letter 'M' you could see, and so on with all the other letters; and when she had finished –

'Now,' said the little man, smiling, 'you see you didn't fill up the page after all.'

'Then put in another basketful of kisses to mother,' said Monona – 'half for me and half for you.'

Gladys did, and then the little man gave her a tiny envelope.

'But how are we to send the letter?' asked Monona.

The little man, instead of answering her, cocked up his eye, and said:

'I saw you all the time, my gay buccaneer,' said he, 'with your head on one side, and you listening to every word the young ladies and myself have been saying.'

The children looked up, and what should they see on a branch over their heads but a robineen, and he looked as bold as you please.

'Take this,' said the little man, handing up the envelope to him, 'and be off with you!'

The robineen caught it in his beak, and away he flew.

'But how will he know where to go?' asked Gladys.

'He knows the place as well as yourself, my lady,' said the little man. 'Don't you remember putting the crumbs on the window-sill in the winter,' said he, 'and the robineen that used to pop on to it and peck away as if he hadn't a bit to eat for a twelvemonth?'

'And was that he?' said Monona.

'The very same,' said the little man, 'but he's

got so stout now that you'd hardly know him. Now if you're coming with me, let us go,' said the little man, and the three of them stepped along the branch until they came to the little door in the tree.

'All you have to do is to slidder down,' said the little man, and down they all slid together, and when they got out below, what was there waiting for the girleens but two little horses not much bigger than greyhounds? One was as black as the wing of a raven, and one was as white as driven snow, and the black one had golden shoes, and the white silver ones. Gladys jumped up on the white and Monona on the black.

'That's right,' said the little man, 'I wish I could go with you, but you know I must stay here to mind the door. All you have to do is to sit still, and the little horses will take you to the Fairy Queen's Palace; but don't stop them a second, for if you do you'll never get there.'

And kissing hands to the little man, off the children galloped, and they thought the little steeds were treading on air, and no wonder, for the blades of grass didn't give way under the little hooves. It was not long till they were galloping over a mossy pathway through a great forest, when, lo! in a little glade what should the children see but a little red man!

He was all in red, from the top of his head to the shoes on his feet. His head was red, and his eyebrows were red, and the little buttons on his jacket and the little buckles on his shoes were all of red gold. What was he doing but standing on his head and tossing up in the air with the soles of his feet ten little golden balls that, as they rose and fell, struck against each other, making the most musical sound that ever you heard. So wonderfully sweet was it that you felt you could stay listening to it all the day long; and the children, forgetting the advice of the little door-keeper, stopped their little horses to look and listen, till their hearts were filled with wonder and delight. Suddenly they were startled by a frightful barking and miowing, and what should sweep past them like the wind but the two hunters of the Woods of Darkness. One of them was a dog by day and a cat by night, and the other was a cat by day and a dog by night.

The little steeds were so frightened that they reared, and the children slipped off them, and away the little horses went through the wood. The little man had vanished like a spark of fire, and when the children recovered from their

fright, they did not know what to do or where to go.

But just then Gladys saw that the little red juggler had dropped three of the little gold balls, and these were hopping along of themselves and striking against each other, giving out the same delightful sounds as before, and the children were so taken with the music that they forgot their plight, and they followed on after the balls, and these hopped, and hopped, and hopped, until they came to a little cottage all covered with ivy, and its door was open, and in through the door the balls bounded.

The children stood as if they didn't like to follow them into the house; but in a second, out came a little woman no higher than your knee. She wore a little white cap, and a little black dress, and she had little gold spectacles on her nose, and she had so sweet-looking a face that anyone would trust her. She bade the children a hundred thousand welcomes, and she brought them inside, and she gave them such cakes and such fruit as were not found anywhere out of Fairyland.

While Gladys was biting into a delicious peach, she happened to look up towards the roof of the cottage, and whom should she see sitting on a beam near the rafters but the Little Red Juggler. She was going to call out, but the little man put his hand on his lip and shook his head solemnly, and she knew he did not wish her to speak.

The little woman kept on pressing the children to eat.

'Eat, my little dears, 'twill do you both good, and that delicious fruit will improve your flavour.'

'Our complexion, you mean. Mother says fruit does that,' said Gladys.

'Oh, of course, your complexion, that's what I meant,' said the little woman, but she reddened up to the two eyes; and Gladys happened again to catch the eye of the Little Red Juggler, and again he shook his head very solemnly.

Well, the children had to stop eating at last, and then Monona said she'd like to go home to Mammy.

'Go home to Mammy! Ho! ho!' laughed the little woman, 'of course you would, and so you will too, ho! ho!' and the little woman kept on laughing as if it were the funniest thing in the world. The children laughed too, though they didn't know why, and then the little woman caught Monona and tickled her until she got a fit of the giggles.

'But now, my dears,' said the little woman, 'stay here and wait till I come back; I'm going out into the forest to get wood for the fire for my son's supper.'

Before they could answer, she had passed out and locked the door behind her. The children began to get frightened, when down jumped the Little Red Juggler to the floor.

'My poor little children,' he said, 'you don't know where you are at all, at all. That little woman, for all that she looks so sweet, is a cruel Witch, and she means to give the both of you to her son tonight for his supper. One of you will be roasted, and one boiled,' said the Little Juggler.

When they heard this, the children threw themselves into each other's arms and began to cry.

'Crying is no use, my dears,' said the Little Red Juggler, 'and 'twill spoil your eyes,' said he, 'but if you will be said by me I'll save the two of you.'

'We'll do anything you tell us,' said the children.

'Well, then,' said he, 'one of you must go into the next room and get the black-hafted knife that is on the window-sill. I dare not go into the room, for I'm under bonds to the Giant – that is the Witch's son – not to do it, and what's more, if I did go in, my feet would stick to the ground, for the Witch has put enchantments on it.'

'Maybe I'd stick there too,' said Gladys.

'Oh no,' said the little man, 'I wouldn't send you in if you would, for how could you bring me out the knife if you got stuck?'

'That's true,' said Gladys, and without another word she darted into the room, and brought back the knife.

'Now,' said the Little Juggler, 'I'll put my head on the table, and you must cut the head off me.'

But Gladys dropped the knife on the table, and said she couldn't, and she wouldn't, and she wouldn't.

'Well, you'll do it, womaneen,' said the Juggler, turning towards Monona, but Monona backed away from him and began to cry.

'Oh, stop crying, or I'll cry myself,' said the Little Juggler. 'If you don't cut my head off, maybe you'd cut off my finger.

But the children wouldn't.

'Ah, I was only trying you all the time,' said the little man. 'But one of you must give me a little cut with the knife on the finger and get one drop of blood. That will be enough to free me from the enchantments that are over me.'

'Why don't you do it yourself?' asked Gladys.

''Twouldn't do,' said he. 'It can only be done by a good little maiden that never told a fib.'

'Very well, I'll do it,' said Monona.

'Oh, Monona!' exclaimed Gladys, 'how could you?'

But Monona made a little cut in the Little Red Juggler's finger, and a tiny drop of blood came out, and in a minute the Little Juggler was a fine, tall, handsome young Prince.

'Now, my little darlings,' he said, folding the children in his arms, 'I shall be able to save you from the horrible Giant.'

He had hardly said this when there was a loud knocking at the door.

'Run in there and wait for me,' said the Prince, and the children ran into the next room.

The knocking at the door became louder.

'Open, open, or I'll break it in!' shouted the Giant, for it was he, and wasn't he astonished when the door was opened, and he saw the Prince standing before him?

The howl of rage that he uttered nearly

frightened the children to death, but he never uttered another word, for the Prince had drawn his sword, and though the Giant had a club as big as a small tree, the Prince attacked him, and with one blow swept the head from his shoulders. When he fell, the children heard a horrible screech outside in the forest, and they peeped out of the window and they saw the Hounds of the Woods of Darkness gobbling up the Witch.

Then the Prince came in to them, and he told them that the Giant was killed, and they asked him would he take them home.

'Mammy won't know what's become of us,' said Gladys. 'We told her to wait for us at the tree through which we came to Fairyland.'

'I will, of course,' said the Prince, 'but it is getting too dark to go through the forest tonight, and if you lie down and go to sleep, I'll take you with me in the first light of the morning, and if you are asleep then, I won't waken you,' said he, 'but I'll carry you to mother.'

The children were so tired that they fell sound asleep, and never wakened when the Prince took them up the next morning and carried them through the forest.

He went up through the tree down which they had come, and there outside the little door

Mammy was waiting. He put the children down beside her, and when they woke up they saw their mother bending over them.

'Shaun of the Leaf'

Once upon a time there lived in a house near a great forest, two little children named Donal and Eily. They had been very, very happy until a stepmother came over them, who could not bear to have them in her sight. She hunted them out of the house during the day, and packed them off to bed as early as possible and often without their supper, and they were no longer allowed to sit up to hear the songs of the wandering harpers or the stories of the bright beautiful fairyland over the sea, where all were young and ever free from sorrow. Their dear old nurse, who loved them better than she loved herself, was sent away, and their father took hardly any notice of them, and the servants treated them almost as badly as the stepmother did herself.

They had only one friend in the world, and this was the dog 'Bran', a big, shaggy wolf-dog, that always slept beside their bed at night, and, when he had time, used to go with them, and show them the way into the wood when they desired to play there.

One day, when the stepmother was very, very cruel to them, they went to the wood and sat down under a large tree and began to cry. Bran looked at them very sorrowfully for a while, and then put his face up to theirs and whined as if he were crying too.

'Poor Bran,' said Eily. 'What would we do without you?'

Bran shook his head three times, as much as to say, what would he do without them, and then he pulled Donal by the sleeve and ran away four or five steps, and came back again and gave Donal another pull.

'He wants us to go with him,' said Eily.

Bran wagged his tail and barked three times, as much as to say 'you are right'. Then the children rose, and Bran ran on before them, but he turned round every minute to see if they were following him. He went on and on, and Donal and Eily after him, until they came to a grassy, open place in the wood.

In the middle of this, lying on the ground, was a big tree blown down by a storm, and sitting on the tree, was a little man in a frieze coat, with tails that came down to his heels and knee-breeches with brass buttons, and he had

an ivy-leaf up to his lips, and on it he was playing very sweetly, but in so low a note, that he
could scarcely be heard. Bran and Donal and
Eily were very close to him before he saw them.
When he did, he stopped playing, and, jumping
down from the tree and pushing his spectacles
up on his forehead, he cried out:

'How are you, Eily and Bran and Donal? 'Tis
I that am glad to see you, and many's the time I
saw ye when ye weren't thinking of me.'

When Bran heard his name he barked and
danced for joy, and he would have jumped up
on the little man only he was afraid of knocking
him down. Eily and Donal did not know what
to make of it all, and they couldn't guess how
the little man knew their names. But all the
same, they said:

'Very well, thank you sir.'

'I see you don't know who I am, Donal and
Eily,' said the little man; 'but Bran remembers
me, don't you, Bran?' said he, winking at the
dog in a way that would do your heart good to
see.

Bran was so delighted that he stood straight
up on his hind legs, but overbalancing himself
he fell on the broad of his back, and the little
man and Donal and Eily shook their sides

laughing at him.

'But I must tell you who I am,' said the little man to Donal and Eily. 'Don't you remember "Shaun of the Leaf" as they used to call him, that often and often sat by the fire in your house, and played many a tune for you, and told you many a story?'

'That used to tell us the stories of the bright fairyland, where everyone is happy,' said Eily, looking sharply at the little man.

'Yes,' said the little man.

'Of course, we remember him; we never forgot him,' said Eily.

'Well, then, I am he,' said the little man, 'I am he – I am "Shaun of the Leaf", and I have just come from the land I used to tell you about,' said Shaun, taking out a tortoise-shell snuff-box and treating himself to a pinch.

'But, I thought it was only the fairies lived there,' said Eily.

'Well, it is only fairies live there, except myself, and for that matter I'm nearly a fairy myself now,' said Shaun. 'I was playing here one summer's evening in this very spot, trying to take off the notes of the thrush and the blackbird, when who should come by but the King and Queen of the Fairies, and a lot of the quality attending them, and they took such a fancy to the music that the queen asked the king to invite me down to their palace under the sea; and they made such fine promises – and I was willing to do anything to oblige a lady, not to say the Queen of the Fairies herself – I consented, and I am as happy as the day is long.'

'But sure you were a great big man when you used to come to our house,' said Donal.

'I was six feet high in my stockings then,' said Shaun, and he drew himself up very proudly, and he took another pinch of snuff, 'but you know I had to become small, or I couldn't go into the Fairy King's Palace.'

'Was it the fairies made you small?' asked Eily.

'It was,' said Shaun.

'And how did they do it? said Donal.

'Boiled me – boiled me down,' said Shaun.

'Boiled you!' exclaimed Eily, and her eyes got nearly as big as saucers.

'They put me to simmer for two hours over a slow fire,' said Shaun, solemnly.

'In a pot?' said Eily.

'Well, they said it was a cauldron,' said Shaun, 'but between you and me, Miss Eily, not to tell anything but the truth, I think it was a pot.'

'Did they put herbs into it?' asked Donal.

'They did,' said Shaun.

'Then I know what it was, it was a "magic cauldron",' said Donal.

'Maybe so, Donal asthore, but having spent two hours in it, you wouldn't much mind whether they called it a pot or a cauldron,' said Shaun. 'But it's nearly time for me to go home, and I am afraid I did very little practice today.'

'What kind of practice?' said Donal.

'Music,' said Shaun. 'Didn't ye hear me playing when ye came up?'

'We did,' said Eily, 'and we thought it very, very sweet.'

'Oh, then, ye can hear music sweeter this minute,' said he, 'and that is the song of the birds. There are no birds down in the land I told you about, and I have to come up here every fine day when the birds are singing, to try and learn their notes for the king and queen. There's one black bird that sings in the tree near the stream there that almost breaks my heart. But my time is up, and I must go,' said the little man.

'We wish we could go with you,' said Donal, 'for when we go home our cruel stepmother will beat us.'

'Wirrastrue,' said Shaun, 'is that the way at home now? Leave it to me,' said he, 'and I'll tell the Queen of the Fairies, and you may be sure she will take care of you when she learns from me how good your poor mother was to "Shaun of the Leaf". This is Monday, and I can't be back here again until Thursday, as there is a great wedding tomorrow, and the dancing will be kept up for two days and two nights. So come here again on Thursday,' said he, 'and now run home as fast as ye can.'

When he had said this, little 'Shaun of the Leaf' disappeared through the trees. Bran gave a couple of barks to say goodbye, and then started home with Donal and Eily.

When they arrived home the stepmother was trying to light the fire, which had gone out. When she saw Donal and Eily she screamed at them and abused them, and said they were good-for-nothing idlers, roaming about the country instead of staying at home to mind the fire.

'As for you,' said she, throwing a burnt stick at Bran, 'you're not worth the bit you eat.'

Bran snarled and showed his teeth, but Donal and Eily crept into a corner, and said nothing.

That night when they went to bed, they talked about the little man, and were longing for Thursday to come. The next day passed, and the next, and the stepmother's temper was worse than ever. She slapped Eily because she gave a sup of milk to Bran, and boxed Donal's ears and took up the broomstick to beat him because he kissed Eily and asked her not to cry. That night she sent them to bed without their supper – but they did not mind, they knew the next day was Thursday, and talked themselves to sleep, and dreamed all night of 'Shaun of the Leaf', and of the fairy queen they were going to see. When they awoke in the morning the sun was dancing in the room, and one would think all the birds in the air were singing outside the window. They could hear Bran, too, barking away down in the fields.

'Bran is chasing the larks,' said Donal.

'Oh, Donal,' said Eily, 'did you ever hear the birds singing like that before?' They listened and listened, and the birds kept singing, and what they sang was – *Come with me to Tir-na-nÓg* – that is the fairyland where all are young; and the children felt very happy when, after breakfast, the stepmother turned the two of them out. Bran was outside, and when he saw them he gave them a look as much as to say 'follow me', and they set off to the wood. It wasn't long till they came to the place where they were to meet 'Shaun of the Leaf'.

But they could see no sign of him, and Eily and Donal began to feel very sad. However, Bran looked at them and wagged his tail as much as to say 'It's all right.' Sure enough it was not long until they heard Shaun playing on the ivy leaf, and soon they saw him pushing his way through the ferns.

'I'm sorry for keeping you, Eily and Donal and Bran,' said he, 'but I have good news for you. The Queen of the Fairies sent me up to tell you that she's dying to see the two of you, and she wants you to come to her this very day.'

When Bran heard this, his head hung down to the ground; but when Eily saw Bran, she took pity on him and said:

'Can't Bran come too?'

'Well,' said the little man, 'I didn't get an invitation for Bran, because I thought he wouldn't care to come, for there are no birds to hunt there, you know.'

Bran straightened himself up and gave a low growl, as much as to say: 'As if I wouldn't rather be near Eily then have all the birds in the world.'

'But I'll put in a good word for Bran,' said he, 'with the Queen of the Fairies, and I'm sure she'll let him come to the palace; but at present he must stop at the house of the friend where my horse is stabled.'

Eily and Donal agreed to this, and so, too, you may be sure, did Bran, who began to bark and jump about like mad.

'Stop, now, for a minute or two,' said the little man, 'till I take off that blackbird's note, and I'll be ready to go with you.'

Shaun sat down on the tree, and, closing his eyes, his head rested on his left shoulder, and he played so softly on the leaf that Eily could hardly hear him.

'I have it at last,' said the little man, starting up, his face beaming with delight. 'And now come with me to Tir-na-nÓg.'

He sang the very song the birds had been singing that morning when the children were listening to them!

'Shaun of the Leaf' went before them, pushing aside the ferns. Eily and Donal followed. Soon they passed through the wood. A broad plain was before them, and beyond the plain the sea shining like silver. When Shaun passed out of the wood, he began the play upon the leaf, and so sweet was the music that Eily thought it was only a minute until they came to the sea.

As soon as they came to the strand, what did they see coming around the rocks and swimming gracefully along but a beautiful snow-white swan, with a gold bridle and a saddle of purple and gold.

'Is this your horse?' said Donal, his eyes opening wide in wonder.

'He is,' said Shaun, 'my sea-horse you know,' said he, winking at Eily. And in a second after, they saw a tiny boat with six little sailors and little red tassels in their caps coming in to the strand.

'Oh, what is this for? cried Donal.

'That is to take you and Eily to the little green isle in the sea, where the pleasant land of youth is,' said Shaun.

'But that tiny little boat won't hold us,' said Eily.

'Oh, wait till you see,' said Shaun, and when the little boat slid in on the strand, the little sailors with little red tassels in their caps, asked the children to get in.

When Donal and Eily got in, they had plenty of room, although the boat didn't get a bit

bigger; and then the little sailors got in, and 'Shaun of the Leaf' got up in the saddle of the swan and gave the word to start.

'Bow, wow, wow, wow!' cried Bran, when he saw the boat and the swan leaving him.

'Oh, stop, dear sailors, and take in Bran,' said the children.

'He'd sink the boat,' they said. 'We cannot take a four-footed animal into a fairy boat.'

'But Bran can walk on his two hind legs,' said Eily.

'But he has four legs all the same, and he would drown us,' said the little sailors.

'Bow, wow, wow, wow, wow!' barked Bran.

'Oh, we must go back,' said Eily. 'We can't leave poor Bran behind, for mother told us never to go out without him'; and Eily began to cry, and she was sobbing until she heard a voice calling: 'Bran, you goose, swim out and catch the swan's tail.' Then Eily looked, and what did she see but a mermaid sitting on the rocks plaiting her golden tresses.

Bran, barking joyously, plunged into the sea, and tried to catch the swan's tail. The swan got such a fright that she opened her wings, and then she threw Shaun head over heels into the water, and he would certainly have been drowned, if Bran hadn't caught him by his little frieze coat.

'Well, it is not you are to blame, Bran, if I was nearly drowned,' said Shaun, 'and I must admit that you have saved my life, and so if you promise not to touch the swan, you can swim quietly after us, and I'll make it all right for you with the Fairy Queen.'

The swan had come back and let Shaun get up again, and then said Shaun, turning round and shaking his fist at the mermaid: 'I'll pay you off for this yet.' But she only answered with a laugh, and blowing a kiss from the tips of her white fingers, dived into the sea.

And were not the children delighted watching the beautiful swan and Bran swimming close beside them, and the little fairy sailors rowing away with their tiny oars!

But after a while they began to look out for the little green isle in the sea, and they could not catch a glimpse of it anywhere.

'Oh, look, look, Donal! What is that?' shouted Eily, her face aglow, as she stood up in the boat and pointed in the direction to which it was going.

''Tis, 'tis – oh, I really think it must be a

bundle of sunbeams,' said Donal, 'that has fallen on the waters.'

''Tis the true word you spoke, Master Donal,' said 'Shaun of the Leaf', 'a bundle of sunbeams it is, for it is the head of herself, and no mistake,' said he.

'Who is herself?' asked Eily.

'Who would it be, but that deludherin mermaid that you saw on the rocks beyond,' said Shaun.

And sure enough it was the mermaid!

When she lifted her head above the waters, her tossing golden tresses brightened them like dancing sunbeams, and never was sea foam half so white as her white shoulders, and her round white arms.

Higher still she raised herself, until the children saw that she had in her hands a little harp of gold, and as they watched her with all their eyes, they saw her stringing it with strings woven with her own shining tresses.

Then she began to play, and oh! for the music that came out of that little harp of gold.

It stole across the waters to the ears of the children, and crept down into their little hearts; and they hardly noticed the movement of the oars as the little sailors rowed on and on in search of the little green isle in the sea. They barely saw the sea itself, for they could do nothing but listen and listen, and they thought that never had sweeter sounds been heard anywhere in the world.

'Wait till you hear her sing,' whispered 'Shaun of the Leaf', who was able to guess what the children were thinking of. 'Wait till you hear her sing.'

He had no sooner said the word, than the mermaid began to sing.

The little sailors had kept time softly with their oars, to the music of the little harp of gold, but when the first notes of the strange sweet voice fell on their ears, they ceased rowing as if some spell of enchantment had fallen on them. The little boat stood, and the waters became motionless.

The children thought it was all a lovely dream, from which they were awakened by a long deep-drawn sigh from 'Shaun of the Leaf'.

'What are you sighing for?' asked Eily.

'Musha, then, it is no wonder I'd sigh, for sure I never hear her voice that it does not coax the heart out of me, and I'm not worth a pin for a month of Sundays after, and she does not care a thraneen about me,' said he, with another sigh that would almost bring the tears to your eyes.

A merry laugh rippled along the waters, and the children saw the mermaid waving her white arm to them, and then she sank beneath the sea; but for a while there lingered on its surface the glistening of her golden hair, as the golden light of the sun that has set often lingers in the evening skies.

Then all at once the little sailors began to ply their oars, and soon the little boat was sliding over the circles in the water which told where the mermaid had gone down. They had no sooner passed beyond the circles than the children saw before them the little green isle in the sea.

Well, it was not long till the boat ran in on the brown sand, and the little sailors jumped ashore and handed out the children.

'I was here as soon as yourself,' said the little man, jumping off his feather sea-horse, which had just stepped on the strand.

'Oh, Bran, mind what you are doing, you naughty dog!' cried out Eily.

For there was Master Bran, shaking himself for the bare life; and he had very nearly made a mess over Eily, owing to the showers of water he flung on her.

'I knew it was not right to bring dogs here,' said the little man. He whisked out his snuff-box and took two pinches.

'Bow, wow, wow, wow, wow!' barked Bran.

'Who is that barking?' said the Fairy Queen, who had just come down a pathway all covered with bluebells that made a carpet under her tiny feet.

When Bran heard her he hung down his head and looked very sorrowful, as if he was thinking of saying: 'I beg pardon, your majesty,' and he got behind the children to hide himself.

When Donal and Eily saw the Queen, they were so dazzled with her beauty that they could not speak for wonder. But the Fairy Queen came over and put her arms round Eily, and kissed her and hugged her, and then kissed and hugged Donal, and said: 'A hundred thousand welcomes to Tir-na-nÓg.' Then she brought them into the palace, and all the little fairies came thronging around them, and made them welcome. Then there was a grand feast, and after that there were games of all kinds and dancing, and no two children were ever so happy as Donal and Eily.

But in the middle of the dance the little

trumpeters on the battlements of the palace sounded a note of warning, and the music ceased, and the dancers stayed their steps.

A little herald, dressed in brown silk, entered the ballroom.

'What message do you bring, O Herald?' said the Fairy Queen.

'The Fairies of the Sea, your Majesty,' said the herald, bowing almost to the ground, 'challenge the Land Fairies to battle.'

'Bid the trumpets blow,' said the Queen to her attendants, 'to announce that we accept their challenge, and you, my gallant knights, get you ready for the fray.'

The ballroom was emptied in the twinkling of an eye.

'Come down with me to the strand,' said 'Shaun of the Leaf' to the children, 'and we'll see the fight.'

The children went down with him to the strand, and they looked out upon the sea; but they had at once to put their hands to their eyes to shade them from the dazzling light that flashed from its countless ripples, for every ripple bore along a glancing Sea Fairy, whose little coat was studded all over with shining pearls.

'Look behind you,' said 'Shaun of the Leaf' to the children, 'and rest your eyes.' Donal and Eily looked behind them, and saw descending the grassy slopes that bent towards the strand the fairest sight that ever mortal eyes beheld.

Regiment after regiment of little Land Fairies were marching down, and they looked like a garden of moving flowers.

The first carried in their hands poppies nearly as red as the heart of the rose, the second bore bunches of cowslips nearly as golden as the heart of the sun, and after them came the wild roses of the hedges, white and red, and as lovely as the cheeks of little girls, and the bluebells from the woods came after, and nearly every flower that grows all through the year followed. For this is the way the battles were carried on between the Land Fairies and the Sea Fairies.

The Land Fairies fought with flowers and the Sea Fairies with pearls. The Land Fairies rushed out towards the incoming wave, and flung their flowers against the Sea Fairies, but woe betide them, if while doing so, the tips of their toes went into the water, for if they did, they became prisoners and servants of the Sea Fairies, for a year and a day.

79

The Sea Fairies, casting their pearls, skimmed along the wave, until they came to the very edge of the strand, but woe betide them if the tips of their toes touched the dry sand, for if they did, they became prisoners and servants of the Land Fairies for a year and a day.

Well, the battle had hardly begun, when the edge of the sea was a mass of fragrant flowers, and the edge of the strand was white with shining pearls, and the shouts of the little combatants filled the air, and many prisoners were taken on both sides.

'Donal,' said Eily, 'wouldn't you like to play?' – for the children thought it was all play.

'I would,' said Donal, and before little 'Shaun of the Leaf' could say a word the children had their boots and stockings off, and they were out in the water, and they thought they never had such fun.

They used to catch up a whole armful of the Sea Fairies, but the merry little fellows slipped out from under the children's arms as water slips throught the fingers, and they pelted them with pearls, and Donal, and Eily followed them out till the water got deeper and deeper.

'Come back! Come back!' cried 'Shaun of the Leaf', but the children did not hear, or, if they did, they did not heed him. But at last Eily found she was going out too far, and she wanted to turn back, but she couldn't, for the little Sea Fairies had fastened round her a rope of pearls and they were drawing her along.

'Oh, Donal! Save me!' she cried, but Donal was a prisoner himself and could do nothing; the Sea Fairies were also drawing him far out from the little green isle in the sea, and goodness knows what would have happened to the children, if the Fairy Queen had not come down to the strand in time to see their plight.

'Shaun, Shaun!' she cried, 'go out after the children and bring them back.'

'I dare not do it, your Majesty,' said Shaun, 'for I can't swim. The last time the Sea Fairies caught a hold of me they nearly drowned me, and sure 'twould be no use for me to get drowned, though I'd give my life to save Eily's little finger.'

'I know that, Shaun,' said the Queen.

Then the Fairy Queen ordered the little sailors to go out and save the children, and they pushed out their little boat. They rowed and they rowed, and it was not long until they came close to the children, and some of them stretched out their hands to take Donal and Eily in when a crowd of little Sea Fairies climbed up the sides of the boat and tumbled into it, and at last so many came in that they swamped it, and all that the Fairy Queen could see of her little sailors was their little red caps floating on the top of the water.

'Oh, what will I do at all, at all,' said the Fairy Queen, 'if the children are carried away.'

She wrung her hands, and never before was she so sorry, for she loved the children for themselves as well as for their sweet mother's sake.

'I know what we'll do,' said little 'Shaun of the Leaf', for he, too, had been very miserable.

'What is it?' said the Queen.

'Let us call Bran,' said he, and he whistled, and down came Bran with a bound. He had been sitting up on a sand hill all the time longing to join Donal and Eily, but he was afraid of the Fairy Queen.

Shaun pointed to the children. 'Bring them back, Bran,' he said, and out went Bran. He plunged into the waves, and, resting his chin on the waters, he swam, and he swam, until he came up to Eily. The little Sea Fairies scattered before him as the minnows scatter before a pike, but one of the Fairies, bolder than the others, tried to fling a rope of pearls around Bran's neck, but Bran showed his white teeth – whiter than the pearls – snapped at the Fairy, and nearly gobbled him up. This so frightened all the rest of the Fairies, that they dived under the sea.

Bran was just in time to catch Eily, and Donal was close enough to fling his arm over Bran's neck and grasp his shaggy hair, and the gallant wolf-dog brought the children safely back to the strand.

'Oh, Bran, Bran!' said the Fairy Queen, when he had brought her back the children safe and sound, 'you may bark as much as ever you like now.'

And didn't Bran bark! And didn't he caper, and didn't he shake himself, and fling showers about him on every side!

Then the Queen hurried the children to the palace, for they were wet through, and her little maids of honour attended to Eily, and they took off her clothes, and gave her a lovely bath, and they wiped her dry in gossamer, and they laid her down on the daintiest little bed that ever was. It was as soft as air, and as sweet as roses. The gentlemen of the Fairy King's bed-chamber (the King himself was away on a visit to the High King of Erin, at Tara) attended to Donal. Then what did the Queen do, lest the children might feel lonely or frightened if they woke in the dark, but send one of her little fairies up to the sky for a little green star, and she hung this for a night-light on the wall of their dainty bedroom. But the children were no sooner in bed than they fell fast asleep, and did not wake till morning.

Then the Fairy Queen went herself and helped them to get up and dress, and she hugged them, and hugged them, and said she wished she could keep them to herself. But she had promised their mother that she would look after them at home, and she had brought them to Tir-na-nÓg only that she might give them, with her own hands, a little present that would rid them of all their troubles and sorrows.

She took out of her pocket a little crystal flask, and in this was a red-coloured fluid. She held it up to the light, and it shone like a ruby, and she told Donal, as she handed it to him, to throw some of it over his stepmother the next time she attempted to strike him. Then she gave the children a fairy breakfast, and such a breakfast, but there is no use in trying to tell what it was like to anyone who was never in Fairyland.

After this, the Queen, attended by all her maids of honour, accompanied the children down to the strand. Here she bade them a fond goodbye, and Shaun and the little boat and the sailors were on the shore waiting for them; and Donal and Eily were very sorry when they got into the boat and turned their backs on Fairyland, and very frightened they were when they came near to their father's house, for they knew their stepmother would beat them. And so it happened. The moment she caught sight of them she rushed out with the broomstick and made a blow at Donal, shrieking:

'Where have you been, you villians?'

But Donal avoided the blow, and taking off the gold top of the flask, he flung the red fluid on her. He had no sooner done so that she uttered a horrible screech, and on the spot she was changed into a witch-wolf. And all the dogs, with Bran at their head, rushed at her as she sprang out of the farmyard and fled off howling towards the forest.

She was a witch, and she had put a spell on their father. But, after he had found this out, he was never unkind to the children any more, and although they often thought of Fairyland, they lived very happily ever after. And you may be sure they never forgot their dear old Bran.

Irish Folk Stories for Children

T. Crofton Croker

These exciting and spell-binding stories are full of magical people and enchanted places which will delight and entertain children of all ages. *Irish Folk Stories for Children* are tales of past centuries when magic and mystery were part of everyone's life. They include such well loved stories as 'The Giant's Stairs', 'The Legend of Bottle-Hill' and 'The Soul Cages'.

Irish Legends for Children

Lady Gregory

Irish Legends for Children is a heart-warming collection of exciting stories which will give all children hours of pleasure as they catch the flavour and atmosphere of ancient times.

These traditional legends, which have been handed down through countless generations, are written in a direct and simple style and include such well-loved tales as 'The Children of Lir','The Coming of Finn', 'Finn's Household' and 'The Best Men of the Fianna'.

Irish Fairy Tales

Edmund Leamy

In writing these fascinating stories Edmund Leamy turned to our Gaelic past to give the Irish people something which would implant in them a love for the beauty and dignity of their country's traditions.

'Princess Finola and the Dwarf' is a tale so filled with simple beauty and tenderness and there is so much genuine word-magic in it that one is carried away under its spell. All of the stories reveal the poetry of the author's style and show how charged they are with qualities which are peculiar to the Gaelic temperament. At times there is a simple, sweet beauty of language and some passages — especially in 'The Huntsman's Son' — of true prose poetry.

The other spell-binding tales in this book are 'The Fairy Tree of Dooros', 'The House in the Lake', 'The Little White Cat', 'The Golden Spears' and 'The Enchanted Cave'.

No one can read these pages without feeling the charm of a fine delicate fancy, a rare power of poetic expression and a truly Irish instinct.